THE GRIEF WAVE

Written, illustrated & designed by **Trace Moroney**

Someone I really love … has died.

Died.

I am not sure what this means, and I am confused by the feelings churning around inside of me.

I feel shocked, scared, angry, worried, upset, tired … and very, *very*, *very* sad.
My tummy feels sick and my heart is achy …
and I just don't feel like doing
the things I normally do.

Others call it **grief**.

Go away
I don't wa
to play

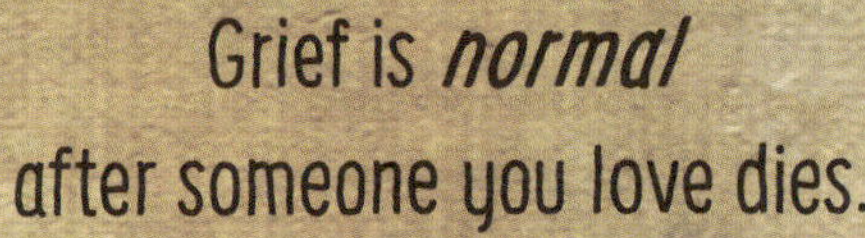

Grief is ***normal***
after someone you love dies.

And grief isn't exactly the same for everyone,
because we are all different.

Grief is the time it takes for us to slowly get used to
the person we loved – not being with us any more.

It is a time for our bodies and minds to
understand that the person who died
is never coming back.

There are many words grown-ups use to describe when someone has died, like …

But these words *really* confuse me.

I need grown-ups to help me understand my confusing feelings by explaining death and dying using simple words in a truthful way, and not be afraid to use the words **died** or **dead**.

Grief feels like being swept away by
a great, big, **gigantic**
wave of sadness …

tumbling my feelings around and around, inside-out and upside-down!

When the grief wave has passed
and the painful feelings have calmed down,
I feel exhausted and empty
and confused
and
alone.

Grief can make my brain feel fuzzy
and it can be hard to know what I want.

Sometimes, I want to be on my own –
and other times I want to hold on tight to someone.
Sometimes, I want to cry and cry and cry –
and other times I can't seem to cry at all.
Sometimes, I want to talk about the person who died –
and other times I don't want to talk at all.

And sometimes, I just want to forget these
topsy-turvy feelings –
and laugh and play for a little while.

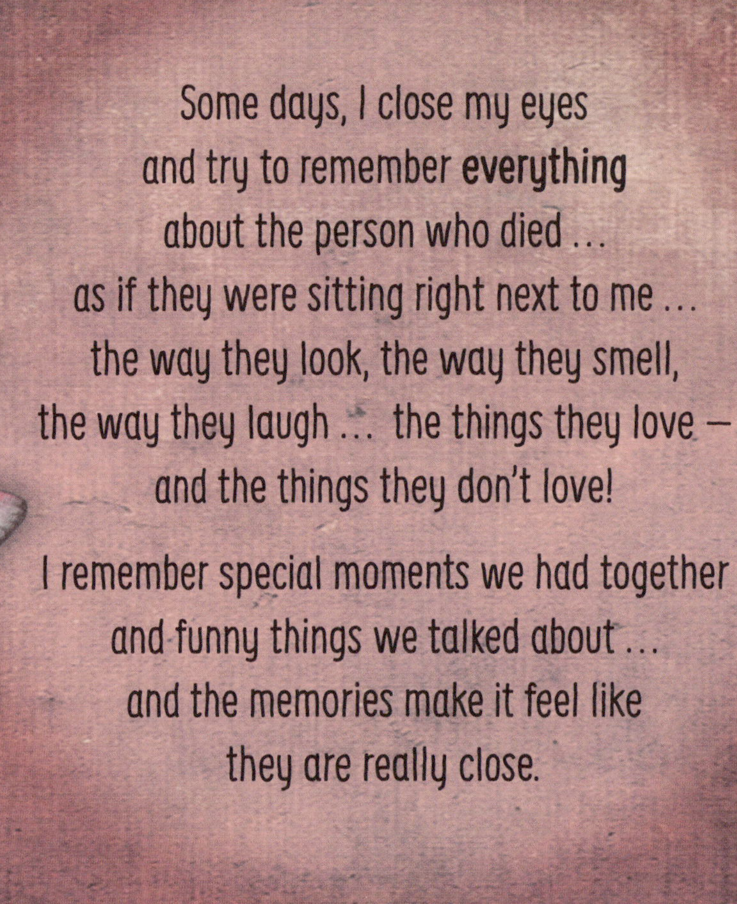

Some days, I close my eyes
and try to remember **everything**
about the person who died ...
as if they were sitting right next to me ...
the way they look, the way they smell,
the way they laugh ... the things they love –
– and the things they don't love!

I remember special moments we had together
and funny things we talked about ...
and the memories make it feel like
they are really close.

And sometimes, I forget they have died and are not here anymore …
until … out of nowhere, another grief wave sweeps over me.
This time though, it is a little bit smaller. And this time
I remember that I was OK after the last grief wave, and
I will be OK after this one too … and the next, and the next.

The grief waves may never, ever go away, but – over time –
they become smaller and easier to cope with.

The grief waves are really hard to understand, but it helps to remember *my feelings are normal* and it's OK to ask a grown-up questions I have, like:

What happens to people when they die?

Why do people die?

Where do they go?

What does DEAD mean?

What is a coffin?

Do they get cold or hungry?

What happens to a dead body?

Will they come back?

What is going to happen to me?

Was it my fault?

Where do they go to the toilet?

I may need to ask these questions again and again,
so please be patient with me.
And it's OK if you say that you 'don't know' the answer,
as this is easier for me to accept and understand
than an answer that is confusing and untrue.

I try to remember to do things that help calm my mind and body, and things that help me feel safe and loved, so that it's easier to cope with the grief waves (and the times in between), like:

Do something physical to get some stress out:
play a sport; play in a park; kick a ball;
run around; stamp my feet; dance;
go for a bike ride; take my dog for a walk;
or play with a pet!

Or do something creative to express my thoughts and feelings:

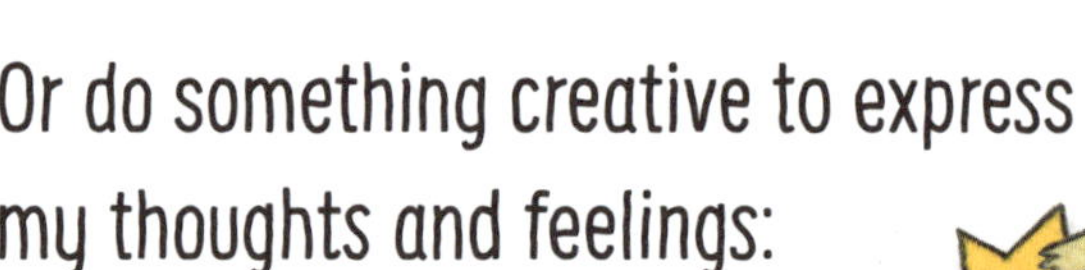

write letters,
poems, or stories;
write in a journal;
draw or paint a picture;
build something;
play or make some music;
or sing.

And get lots of hugs from my family and friends; look after my body by eating healthy food; drink lots of water; try to sleep well (which can be really hard because grief can feel much worse at night); and … be kind and gentle to myself.

Sometimes, the happy memories can feel really sad, but – over time – they do get easier to think about and they help me feel close to the person who died.

Some things I do to remember happy moments are: make a pin-board with photos, special notes and things; plant their favourite tree or flower plant; wear something of theirs; make a special Christmas or house decoration with their name on it; or visit places or do things that we used to do together.

There is a really big, empty space
where the person who died
used to be.

Even though their body isn't here anymore,
the love that I feel for them still is.

So, I like to imagine the big, empty space
is filled with the love we shared…
and that this love will stay
wrapped around me
forever!

Activity: Coping Skills Origami

This easy craft activity is a great way to help you cope with stress and difficult times. You can include your favourite coping skills (learned from this book or created yourself), and once you have made the origami you can play the game which will choose a coping skill you can do to give your brain a break from grief.

You will need:

A square piece of paper; coloured pencils, or crayons, or markers; and a pen or pencil.
Ask for help if you need it!

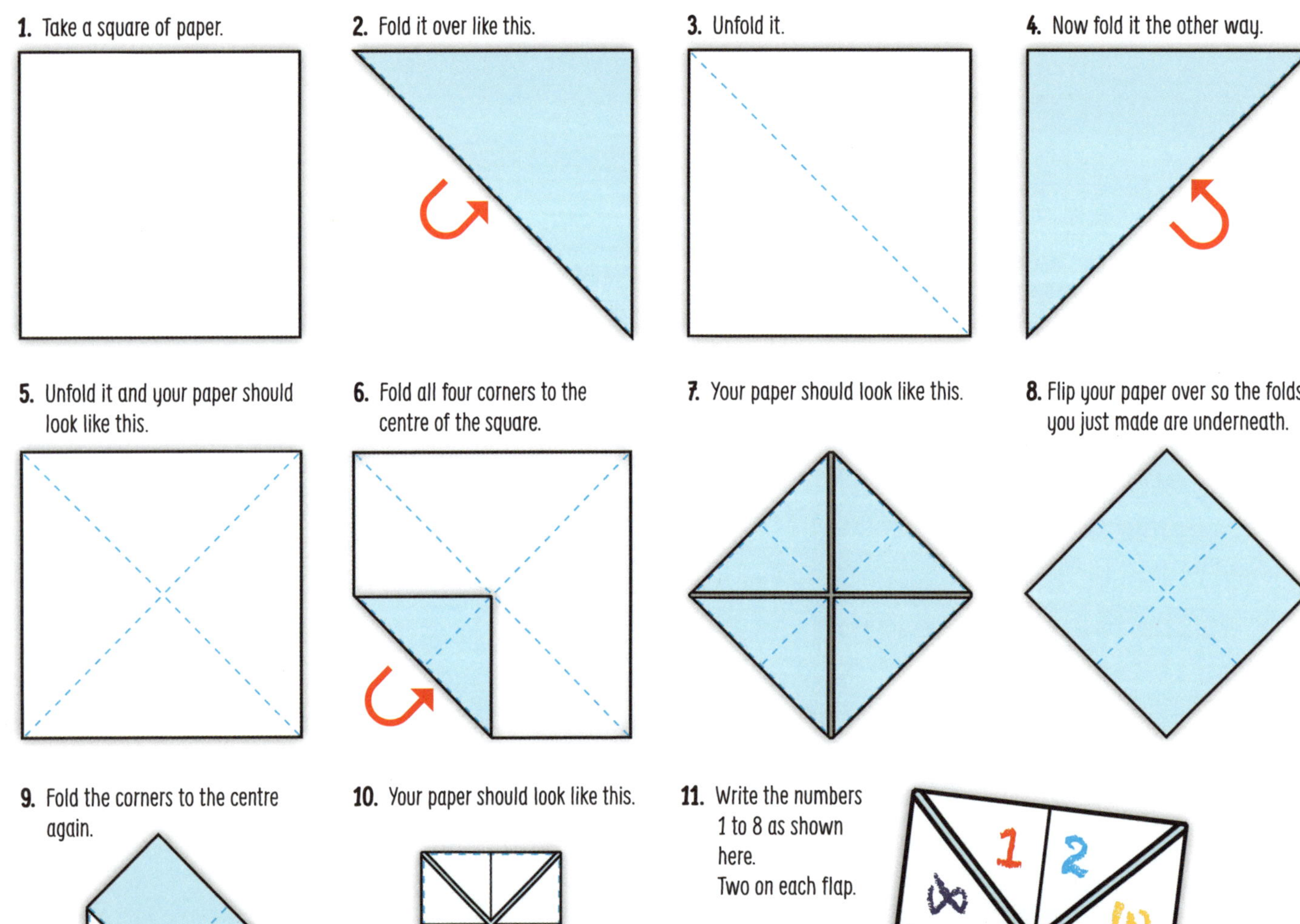

1. Take a square of paper.
2. Fold it over like this.
3. Unfold it.
4. Now fold it the other way.
5. Unfold it and your paper should look like this.
6. Fold all four corners to the centre of the square.
7. Your paper should look like this.
8. Flip your paper over so the folds you just made are underneath.
9. Fold the corners to the centre again.
10. Your paper should look like this.
11. Write the numbers 1 to 8 as shown here. Two on each flap.

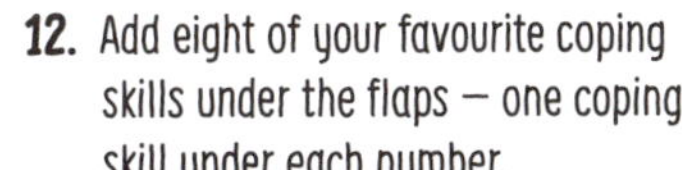

12. Add eight of your favourite coping skills under the flaps — one coping skill under each number.

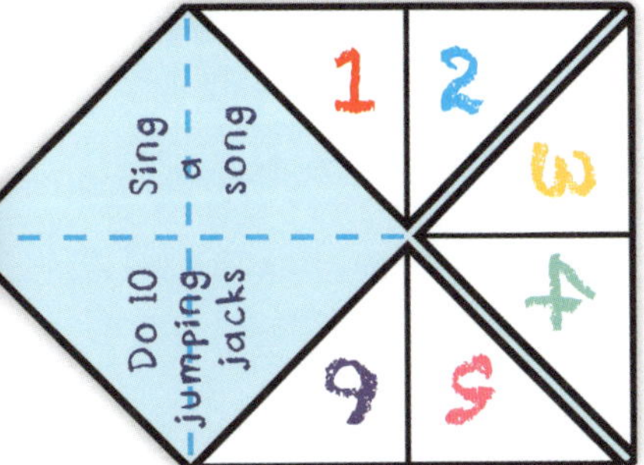

13. Flip your paper over and add a colour or a different object (you can spell out) to each section eg. B-I-R-D.

14. Fold it sideways to crease, then unfold it. Now fold it the other way.

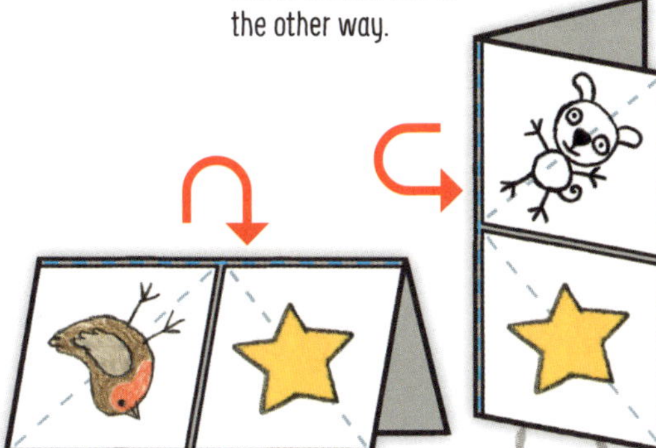

15. Put your index fingers and thumbs under the four open corners.

16. This is what it looks like finished and open.

How to play: You can play this game by yourself, or with someone else. First, choose an object (let's use the BIRD as an example), now spell out the word B-I-R-D and each time you say a letter open and close the origami to the front then the side. On the final letter (D) keep the paper open, then choose a number. Now, open and close the origami (each way) the same number of times as the number you chose. On the final number keep the paper open and choose a number. Open the flap and read the coping skill … now make yourself do it!

Notes to Parents and Caregivers

For many of us, death and dying can be an uncomfortable and difficult aspect of life to discuss – particularly with children. A child's understanding of death is determined by their age, developmental stage, and experience, which is important information that helps us respond in an appropriate and sensitive way to their needs and feelings.

Children in the age range of around 3–9 years old tend to perceive death as a temporary or reversible state – that death is a kind of sleep. They find it hard to understand that death is inevitable and happens to all living things, and may believe that their bad thoughts or behaviour have magically caused or contributed to a death.

Some common grief reactions in children include anxiety; sleep difficulties; anger; self-blame; sadness and longing; misbehaviour; vivid memories; guilt; shame; physical complaints; and problems at school.

Here are some helpful strategies to support your child, and family, through the grief process:

- **Grief is a *process* – and is different for everybody.** There is no right or wrong way to react to the news of a death, or how to express grief throughout the grieving process, providing it is not harmful to self or others.
- Explain death using honest, simple, straight-forward language – with only as much detail as your child is able to understand. Avoid using euphemisms to explain death such as "passed away", "they have gone", or "we have lost them", as these words or phrases can be very confusing and can lead to misunderstanding. Use the correct and direct words in your discussion: dying, death, died, and dead.
- When children feel safe, they ask questions, learn to trust, and share their feelings more readily. Try to answer your child's questions honestly and directly, and check to make sure they understand your explanation. It is OK to say "I don't know". Be prepared for the same question or questions to be repeatedly asked, and for some to be very blunt, or express curiosity about unpleasant details. Reassure and encourage your child to ask questions freely, and while some may make your toes curl with dread – answer them honestly and as best as you can. Your child's questions signify their attempt at trying to understand death. Remember, if you are not part of the immediate family, be respectful to – and consider – the family's set of beliefs and/or belief system when responding to questions.
- Try to maintain usual routines and a familiar environment, and provide lots of reassuring cuddles. Frequently 'check in' with your child, and let them know you are there to comfort them, talk with them, and answer their questions. Remember to acknowledge their feelings and ***actively listen*** to them.

- Provide opportunities for your child to express their feelings through talk, play, and physical or creative activities of their choosing.
- Reassure your child they are safe, secure, and will continue to be loved and cared for.
- Reassure your child that their thoughts, feelings, and behaviour did not cause someone to become ill or to die.
- Ask your child if they would like to participate in remembrance ceremonies (like the funeral, or other rituals that are culturally and spiritually significant for you and your family), and explain what they are likely to expect and experience. Check if they understand your explanation and if they have any questions.
- When someone is in the process of dying (with an illness or old age), it may be helpful to provide your child with an age-appropriate explanation of what is happening, what is going to happen, and why it happens. Remember to be truthful and direct, and do not use euphemisms. Your child, and those surrounding and supporting the dying person may show signs of anticipatory grief (that is, exhibiting grief reactions before – and in anticipation of – the death). This is our body's way of trying to prepare for the eventual death of the dying person, and is a normal part of the grief process.

Grief is commonly described as the process of letting go of the attachment to the person who has died – both intellectually and emotionally. Perhaps a softer way to consider this experience is that grief is the journey from loving someone in their presence – to learning to love them in their absence.

In the context of this book, grief is described in relation to the death of a person. However, for many of us, the death of a much-loved pet can engender similar grief reactions as the death of a much-loved person.

Also, there are many types of ***symbolic losses*** we may experience throughout our lives that can bring about grief reactions such as the loss of the family unit through divorce; loss of friendships; loss of familiar family home or school by moving; separation from parent or primary caregiver; loss of financial status; loss of job; loss of cultural identity; and the loss of health and/or body function. Unfortunately, grief related to a symbolic loss is not often acknowledged.

With effective grief support, we help our children gain valuable skills to manage losses, build resilience, and prepare them to navigate their way through life's inevitable ups and downs.

For more information and support material visit: **www.tracemoroney.com**

For Sophia

The birds of sorrow may rest upon your shoulder,
but don't let them nest in your hair.

Chinese proverb

Published with love by EQ Publications Ltd
email: hello@eqpublications.nz

www.tracemoroney.com
Edited by Madeleine Collinge

Printed in China by
Wai Man Book Binding (China) Ltd.

First published 2021.